Also by Peter Kaufman:

Road Coffee and Selected Stories

The Vetting and Other Stories

Domino=Razzia two Complete Stories

Double Six 12 Themes

Agendas and Choices

Autumn Leaves AND Other Events

Peter Kaufman

AUTUMN LEAVES AND OTHER EVENTS

iUniverse books may be ordered through booksellers or by contacting:

iUniverse
1663 Liberty Drive
Bloomington, IN 47403
www.iuniverse.com
1-800-Authors (1-800-288-4677)

ISBN: 978-1-4917-8271-2 (sc)
ISBN: 978-1-4917-8270-5 (e)

Library of Congress Control Number: 2015918628

Print information available on the last page.

iUniverse rev. date: 1/6/2016

Acknowledgements

Cynthia Kostylo: Front Cover, image, colors art; back Cover, colors, art, photo; internal pages, sketches, images, art; Peter Kaufman: back Cover, book synopsis, author biography, selection of font style, Times New Roman, font size, 12, and author of all poems in *Autumn Leaves and Other Events;* Editing: Brodie, Kaufman, Kostylo, Maxwell; Computer techs: Kostylo, Maxwell---website design and up-grades; Additional research: Fromm, Horney, and my best buddy, Lewis, who was our host to see the Autumn Leaves and Boston during our final visit.

Contents

Autumn Leaves
And
Other Events

Introduction

What Are You Doing

Consider quickness
To outpace the speeding sun,
Through activity
Structured so you cannot see
Incapacity
To accept failure

So, how do you name
Your hidden you,
Do you think:
Commodity, thing
Endless fling
Or, just a process being tested

If you can outwit
The speed of light,
Will all repeated sights
End stress, sleepless nights,
Or in the retrace
Of your choices

Might not some memory, color, sounds
Reveal the real hounds
Biting at your composure
So that no conflicts, doubts,
Daemons, decisions
Still dull your pleasures.

The Lectures: A Novella

Prologue

I've been depressed for a period of time since early in June in 1989 so by September I decide to enroll in more classes at the nearby Junior College for a further change of scene. First, I need to examine what is wearing me down and see what, if anything, I can do about it. Since a new CEO took over in January a couple of years ago, all the news is bad. Obviously, it appears there is little on the surface that can be fixed, moreover, because some of the best new people have already left which makes things worse and forces middle management to try to support a sinking ship. A careful review of every facet of our operation reveals the new CEO's motive; he micro manages, especially where lower level personnel are employed; meanwhile, his micro successes, which collectively amount to macro mistakes, are killing the company. Part of the problem is he believes no one else, but him, is able or competent. Therefore, he always dismisses the experience level of what he considers the lower level, which by definition, are inferior employees. What I face is his idea that cost reduction by firing lower wage employees is a positive cost reduction that improves profit margins, but he is really increasing production failures with the loss of skilled workers necessary to achieve desired results. Second, another problem for me is the state is taking my backyard for the expansion of a new Freeway. The new right-of-way will be right outside my living room window. Yes, I'm depressed.

So, I chose a new program: continue the Poetry class another semester, add a two semester class in Short Story structure and writing and plan to take a new program, to begin in the second semester of 1990, a Philosophy class to be called The Theatre of Ideas; everything to be taught by senior level teachers, like the one who teaches the class in poetry.

Part 1

"Good morning; today we have a surprise guest speaker for our last class before Christmas vacation instead of our regular poetry curriculum. Let me introduce a writer who will impart wisdom, guidance and surprise hints you will not forget as you learn how to improve your poetry and other writing. Since time, our most precious resource is so limited, please no questions. Feel free to take notes, however, and in our classes after Christmas vacation, we will discuss at length today's lecture; your observations, ideas, thoughts, and especially whatever images come to mind, which I look forward to hearing about. Please welcome my long time friend and famous writer, Ray Bradbury."

***

"Thanks for the intro, Lee, and it's great to be here again to speak to poets. I can see from the type of students in front of me that you are still attracting mature, motivated people, so, let's get started: first of all, I'm an idea animal not a Science Fiction writer. You are in this class to learn how to make do---accomplish things. And have fun while doing it; positive fun. I hate the doomsters so I always tell them jokes to loosen them up. Understand, much of what I will say to you is in telegraphic style and it will be up to you to sort it out. Ok, your memories are a resource for you to use; it's how to retrieve them, the memories, are the key. I'll help you do it. One of the answers is friendships, all kinds of them, from relationships to acquaintances: I'm sure each of you has a unique definition of relationship as well as friendship and its friendships which help us sustain our loves not get rid of them; what we want to get rid of are people who doubt us; they are your enemies, not your friends. Don't think of candidates for the honor during our time together, but what I can mention is how to treat negative doubters who want to drag you down.

Next, be aware of what I call cross-pollination; no matter what your field of interest, all your experiences, thoughts, memories and interests transfer into and influence everything about you. For example, I'm reading a poem with Lee that we will give out after class to illustrate my point---I'm not giving it out now because it would interrupt our thoughts as each of you stop to read and analyze it. The poem is by one of Lee's students and may also be included in one of the poems you have discussed so far in this class: the poem is called *Chance and Choice.*

We all need to ask ourselves, 'What roots do we have?' This will help trigger memories, or if you like, another of my terms, 'What will a mid-wife type exposure do for the recall process?' For instance, maybe you recall December 7 1941, (and today is December 7th) and that starts to bring back all sort of memories of what you thought you had forgotten---for me I was doing a play for John Huston called Moby Dick around that time and that brought back all sorts of memories as well as passions of both those moments. However, concentrate on where you are now and take notes for later use.

So, here we are and what sort of mid-wife process can each of you perform to help yourself with memories, passions and the like? This can be done with word association, too, so make list of words then write paragraphs using the words. But remember, this must be a work of fun---and you can also use colors, music and/or the lyrics that go with the music. All of this helps make you a keen observer as well; be aware, too, that often as one writes things come out which are a complete surprise. It happens to me. Now a word of caution, don't push the memory thing, let it occur quietly as you are mining years of the subconscious-well that is inside you. This dredging is almost like meeting yourself.

My scope of interest is vast; I write every day and have for 65 years and have watched the ideas my head links together as I play with them; and to repeat, it's like meeting yourself. When you do this, be alert to Happenstance---which means, especially what is happening by chance, and you just let it transpire. More examples:

I read a poem, an essay or a short story every night which builds my bank of ideas. I just let it percolate in my brain and when I write, it bursts out---actually, I'm simply teaching myself. I will move on, time is limited; your emotions make you survive, then your intellect takes over. I learn from all media: go to art galleries, plays, read everything---even the comics which I've cut out and have saved for years. Just be alert to any place ideas can come from and do it with joy and fun; I never miss any movies and I love Garry Larsen.

Find someone who *loves* you for what you *are* and what you *do*, has intuition; it's done much for me and my creativity---just plunge ahead, do not worry about what you are doing or where you are going, trust your intuition. A word of caution: part of you is private, so do not talk about it. Remember as well: every love affair is a journey, a mystery, an enchantment; and that human work sustains, not political, not religious.

Some final thoughts: things have to be fast, if you slow down, you can ruin things; dry spells come from doing what you should not be doing; your body is telling you to do something else which might be to stuff yourself with data/background to do what you are now attempting. So, be extra alert to any place ideas can come from, also understand you must make a profit (perform) or go out of business.

It's been wonderful talking to you, thanks, Lee, and good luck poets and success in your writing; you have been a great audience."

***

We all expressed our appreciation to Mr. Bradbury for his time and the lecture by standing and applauding. Lee said, "Ray and I are on our way to lunch in the faculty dining-room; he has to leave very quickly and will not have, as I pointed out, any time to answer questions. However, in our next classes we will discuss Ray's presentation and I expect complete cooperation from everyone in the discussion. Be sure to pick up your copy of the poem, *Chance and Choice*. See you all after Christmas vacation on Thursday January 4th, 1990."

The surprise lecture was my last class for the day except for low impact aerobics in the swimming pool. Since I was the student who wrote, *Chance and Choice*, I did not need a copy but collected a copy anyway; however, I found that Lee and Bradbury were looking at another of my poems, too, *The Song;* so after aerobics, I just went home with copies of both poems.

Chance and Choice

Chance and Choice skipping along
Detoured, sat either side of me.
Chance's entreaties spoke to my soul
Of uncertainties, hopes, goals,
That friends, tell friends.
"Choice," I said,
"Can you assure my
Wishes come to pass?"
"Alas," she warned,
"Each his fate must cast
In hand to touch, lips to kiss
Body to caress, be caressed,
But pray, pray,
From the lovers Chance sends,
You chose the friend."

The Song

What is your apprehension?
Why not sing to her desires
Knowing that
Whatever the dimension
Of those fires,
To deter
May only lessen her desire?

But I did commit, just so,
And now, how can you know
The angst I feel
Having sung
Her song,
Only to find
Her gone?

Part 2

I gave my attention to the lecture and Ray's statement that he's an idea person not a Science Fiction writer. I think I understood that the ideas he collects he then uses and makes them into important elements of his stories. Maybe some of the ideas, often, form the background, for part of the plot; the location or the time period of a story. In other words it's ideas which stimulate him and his imagination takes over from there. It's really that he hasn't experienced everything that is in a story but it's this collection of ideas which his imagination and talent use to create and turn it into the final product.

So, I got out one of my loose-leaf, three-hole binder note books and began to analyze my notes, tie them together and see how my efforts might be reflected in images in any poems I'd already written or any future writing I might do. I detected how being organized about writing 'ideas and images' could lead to, maybe, a single story or even two; and I did need help because I'd just accepted an assignment to be the Class Agent responsible for a yearly letter devoted to fund raising. Moreover, even early in my thinking about the job I'd taken, I decided I would not write anything usual but would try-out current topics and make them apply to the importance of fund raising to achieve objectives for the accomplishment of goals not just the grandeur of who raises the most money. (How true my thoughts turned out to be: after 25 years of off-beat letters for the Annual Fund, I turned many of my ideas into short stories. I called them: *Road Coffee*, *Fragile* and *The Bank of Dad*---just three of the 45 stories in my five published books.) But that's another 'story;' it's back to Ray Bradbury's lecture, the notes I took at the lecture and the entries I made in the loose leaf binder books that I filled with the analysis and what I put together from what I believe Ray Bradbury meant in his telegraphic style lecture to all of us.

I put together four of his thoughts: there is cross pollination no matter what your areas of interest or field are; you are here to make things work out, find solutions and how to make do; memories are a resource for you to use, and what I tell you will help you to access and retrieve things; friendships help us sustain our loves, not to get rid of them---however, get rid of people who doubt you: they are not your friends, they are your enemies. This last point made me think: *it wasn't some eccentric CEO who made me feel depressed isolated, it was the people in my private life. They ran down my batteries because they were weak and selfish. They wore away my armor and left me vulnerable and made it seem I was inadequate, not them. So, I asked, why do people pick certain types to be friends with? It was really a question for an experienced psychologist, but indirectly Bradbury triggered it and gave one answer: get rid of people who doubt you.*

The Suitor

That devil Time winked at me
His clock it is that meters the sea.
He bid me, "Wait, be cautious, slow;
Do not the waves in row on row
Always kiss a distant beach?"
So I paused, reflected, did not reach
To touch her lips, her breast, her hand
Nor did I notice on the sand
That Time sat and decoyed the sun
Its downward progress now begun
And before I guessed Time's subtle game,
The watch ran down that held my name.

Verities

Winds
Of perpetual favor
Fill childish daydreams
Till Harmonia wraps us
In pragmatic arms
To tutor the genuine
Reality of life's game:
The price of pleasure
Always includes
Pain.

Part 3

I noticed how the next Poetry class ended with only a brief discussion of Bradbury's lecture. In fact, I was the only student who gave the lecture any attention; so, I soon decided to stop making any comments. Many poetry students had elected to take the Short Story course and our emphasis, therefore, turned this new class into a discussion of how the writers of the 30s and 40s, as well as some writers of today, all start with short stories before they write novels.

I did notice how Ray Bradbury's lecture uses elements writers should employ which contrast poems with the plots/dialogues of Short Stories. I noted, as well, Bradbury talks to poets where he "appears to be 'farming for fodder' for his stories which while they are, in his words, *not Science Fiction*, they are truly a form of myth/fantasy." Regard, as well, Bradbury ties together rules for writing to illustrate how an author reflects/feels about the *impact* of what Bradbury is saying and how an author chooses poems he has written to illustrate Bradbury's 'hidden meaning---true impact' of his content in the lecture. Some examples:

'Be a keen observer
Rid yourself of people who tear-you down, they are enemies
The meaning of cross pollination
Value of money
Value of searching memory for hidden gems in poems
Color/word lists which trigger memory
Music which also triggers memory
Value positive relationships which sustain both
love, us, and do not destroy; see below.
Value of acting fast before idea/image is lost
What you write and how you play with ideas must be fun.
Also, it may be a surprise for you as my
writing and idea-play is for me.
Have a wide array of interests, write every day.'

This is only a partial list from his lecture and other matters will be covered as appropriate.

From the above: why do you hang onto friendships that are negative for you? As a possible clue, recall the number of women (not to pick on woman---this example just came to mind) who form Coffee Klatches. What are some of the common character elements among the members of that group? All are angry, all are divorced, all are shoppers, all are gossips, all want their friends who are unhappy with husband, job, home, level of income, marriage, etc. to join the Klatch and to participate in the bitching, etc.

Find someone who loves just you for what you are and what you do. This is easier said than done for the average individual in our culture. Access to the market place of opportunity, things, people, and so forth is not the same for everyone or the *tempted;* some relationships are like TVs, cell phones, VCRs, sexual partners, clothing, and the like; one does not practice loyalty, commitment, maintenance, with those relationships, one throws them out for a new model.

"Oh, what a tangled web we weave
When first we practice to deceive!"
Marmion, Sir Walter Scott, *(1808)*

The Flirt

Love is the clever one
As she slides easily
Off the tongue
In the moment of passion's
Parting and entrance
Into her dictionary
Of sensual meanings
And sounds,
But it's after the banquet
Of kef exercise and fun,
Where whispered
Alcoholic chatter
Washes the palate
Of your professed,
Joined hip-to-hip,
And tete-a-tete,
That says more.

The Teeter-totter

Psyche balanced
Trust and Love
In a union
So tenuous
That a glance,
Deed or conjecture
Did injure beyond repair
The bond that had fused
Them together,
And so the first to falter
Was Trust
So that Love
Did then implode
And as their sky
Burst from bright to bleak
It left only
Perpetual disbelief
In each other.

Part 4

From my lecture notes, I began to paraphrase and expand some of Ray Bradbury's rapid paced lecture material. At this point, however, he said to us, if I remember it and my notes are correct, 'for your creativity, plunge ahead, do not worry about what you are doing or where you are going with it, trust your intuition'.

I also know he did say, "I am blessed with imagination and intuition and both have done much for me." This made it so clear I thought *a spark of creativity is greater in some than in so many others of us; just like talent---and that while hard work does help, you can't always count on talent which you may not have.* "Sometimes," Bradbury continued, "using one of my memory stimulators will work; for example, *color,* may generate ideas and images especially when I'm writing poetry." "However," as he said in sort of an aside and a cautionary sort of voice, "part of you is private so don't talk about something you do not want to really say and then wish you had been more careful." He did not talk or elaborate on this statement again as if to imply it is up to each of us to decide what is private and confidential and maybe painful experiences will guide us. This is an enigma, too, for me, as writers generally base their output on their life and what they have encountered; how painful some events are that they become so familiar, that perhaps, they should not be mentioned or relived. I know certain family experiences I've been asked to learn and write about which fall into this category. So, should a writer stay away from too sensitive situations that a reader may think reveal more about the author then about a character in the story?

This very enigma came up again when Bradbury said, "Human works, (writings) sustain, not Political, Religious ones." I felt this remark could generate long and heated debate but as a generality, though, I could understand he would seem to be on target to some extent. My notes also include Ray making the point, "things have to be fast to be good; if you slow down, you can ruin things."

I thought right away *maybe that could be when you spoke too quickly and wished later you had thought before speaking!*

I understood his comment about speed to apply to a person's writings, not to the *pace* of a author's personal life, but completely to the *specifics* of a writer's day to day written output. I was partly not wrong, as Bradbury continued, "the pace of a story has to build," but for example, he also added, "every love-affair is a journey, a mystery an enchantment." I thought *this was finally one answer of what to keep private.*

I took this part of his comment to describe someone like Bradbury who must have lived on the edge; who had the money to be in the fast lane and never slow down. Also it would include a Hemmingway type writer, who has the same type: fast, never slow down, personality.

Harmonia

Myths:

The oblong leaves,
Ripened orange hued fruit
Of the Persimmon
Rustle, sway to the winds
Of perpetual, positive favor
As day paints into night.

Shimmering, dancing
Mirages foretell
Sunsets of mutable
Mandarin, the seafarer
Sights as delightful
Devoid of any affrights.

Verities:

A possum stirs at nightfall
Pulpy, vermillion fruit to eat
As a wondrous necklace
Wind fallen is
Created at its feet.

Harmonia importunes
A red warning:
'Pleasure is never absent pain,
It's the price that euphoria
Keeps hidden
But eventually, everyone pays.'

Part 5

The current last class of Lee's poetry class and Christmas Vacation are next; both items remind me of last year and the surprise lecture by Ray Bradbury. Also, it's the end of the first semester in Short Story structure and writing, and to keeping a diary for the second semester to create a short story for class review and comment. So, I check where I am in my notebook of lecture notes and comments. I'm at the Bradbury topic which is Dry Spells in Creativity which my notes begin with his comment, "Dry Spells come from the writer doing what he shouldn't be doing." I thought *this sounds like it is a two phase problem; one is creativity and the other is related, in some manner, to the passage of Time, with a capital T. I relate my thought to a story I was working on about a drinking club founded by some infantry veterans who are unwinding, celebrating their survival in another war and now, which seems common, have become oblivious to Time, by all-out drinking designed to blot-out memories. Their program continues until the club's 'top drinker, Ivor Wallace Harker' gets fed up, takes all his clocks into the backyard and begins to shoot, destroy, all of them, with his M11, especially his battery operated one that displays Time's passage in seconds.*

But back to Bradbury who continues his comment by saying, "the writer is in a rut, not moving fast enough, blocked by surroundings in the wrong Time warp, colors, or sounds, like music; but the biggest cause is not moving fast enough and not stuffing yourself with data, or the background, of what the writer must have, to construct what he needs for his story. Also, the writer may lack money because of failure to make profits or just go out of business." Bradbury continues, "You must become passionate for an idea about which you then write," you ask yourself, 'what are your experiences, what event will act like a mid-wife to help give birth to your goal, get in touch with fun in creating?' Have I lost touch with 'writing must be fun,' being a keen observer, believing, truly believing, really seeing and dredging from the subconscious-well inside me, let a biased way of observing filter out what has never occurred to me before; let memory happen to me, but don't force things. Moreover, cultivate the widest possible interests, write every day, the ideas in your head will link together and then you can play with ideas, but it must be fun', to repeat, "what I have been urging you to do." *It is painful, but is Bradbury also saying, Americans: often spend their entire working lives doing something they dislike and, therefore, lack creative juices. Bradbury is repeating himself but is stressing you have to tell your audience three times or they won't get it.*

I went back to my notes about Time in the story, *Ivor Wallace Harker*, and note Sergeant Harker is telling his buddies, *once Time is burned, it's gone, usually lost forever in memory, especially when Time is not used positively, which is what we are all creating by being drunk every moment of every day and using the lyrics and the music we listen to as augmentation to increase our drinking; our lives, he says, are becoming unreal, illusions.*

Peter Kaufman

Halloween

The simple frights:
Ghouls, goblins, sprites
Must be conquered by maturity
But alas with age
Some still trade the simplicity
Of Halloween's ghosts
For a host of mindless fears
That wisdoms years
Should dissipate.
But we do bargain bogus
Treats and hollow tricks
To contrive a life of delusions,
And when the price is paid,
We ponder our predicament.
And as reality pales, eludes us,
We long for those simpler days
Of jack-o'-lantern illusions.

Tango

Charm did Tango, 'round us
Eluding, tricking with its merry,
Capricious smile, while tempting,
Inviting remembrances of
Light hearted days, where
Wrapped in each moment, were
Rituals: fun, parties, glorious
Intimate nights of dancing
Grasping,
Hugging, loving and
Time.
Oh yes, wondrous Time
We thought would never end!

Part 6

From rereading my lecture notes, I notice a strong connection between Dry Spells and cramming yourself with data, playing with ideas which can link in your head and first, being alert to Happenstance, discovering the unexpected. Early in his lecture Bradbury even gives us a definition: "what happens, by chance, where you let things happen which gives trust and you can even meet yourself."

I thought of a story I wrote for one of my books some time ago about an English MI5 Agent who solves a puzzle everyone has worked on unsuccessfully. The Agent became lost in the maze of one-way-streets in a small city in western Pennsylvania and stops to have lunch in a restaurant called The Tea Room. A group of similarly dressed people are just leaving but the Agent is in time to observe them. He asks the waitress what the letters WCH he sees on their green medical smocks means. She says, 'Westmoreland County Hospital.' In an instant the Agent knows he has the answer to where the twins he is Vetting were born who were found wrapped, abandoned in West Virginia with blankets with WCH on them. His visit to the local County Hospital confirms everything and leads to solving a complex matter.

This exercise in demonstrating, in pinpointing, an important Happenstance I wrote long before hearing Bradbury's lecture, caused me to note *again* a few more of his advices to every writer: "emotion makes you survive and then your intellect takes over; be alert to any place ideas can come from---media, movies, art galleries, museums, chance meetings, a play, new surroundings, and the like; memory joggers especially words, colors, music, even odors from plants, and so forth". I recall Bradbury speaking about what he reads every night and he mentioned essays. I realize that in my new class, The Theatre of Ideas, we have, so far, written essays on Life, Love, Death, Bliss, and another subject, 'follow your heart's path,' where we reviewed a Frost poem, *The Road Not Taken*, as a starting point.

The Apples of Hesperides

Certainly, they are free!
Look how scattered among
Eden's trees
Unguarded, unattended
They hang
Uneaten save by crows
Which peck at their deep,
Golden glow,
Spoiling at random
Row upon row.
So sprint, Atalanta,
Pursue as your
Desire demands,
Tempts you to gather
A fallen few,
Then fly, fly, fly
Seeing, believing
They are free, free, free,
Except for the slavery
Of G*olden* Apples.

Seascape

Recall,
When wave spray
Scatters off the rocks
The fragments portray
A *prism* of colors
In the Autumn sun
And you hurry to capture
A picture's worth
On our picnic basket?
Damn,
You'll never render
The reality you strive for each day
As you repaint, repaint, repaint;
Fool,
Spray colors dry
While you chafe, chafe, chafe,
Just like our wetness
Evaporated, too, when your
Control, control, control,
Harried us into arid oblivion.

Part 7

There are two admonitions that Bradbury gives us that quietly depend on key words: he tells us what we want to do is to get rid of all people who *doubt* us: *Doubt* is the key word in this piece of direction; however, it was stressed as he spoke, so I have highlighted it, as I believe he would have were his lecture printed for us. The second instruction contains a pair of key words to find someone who loves you for what you *are* and what you *do*. Both these words are operational and, once again, they were stressed as he spoke, and I believe would have been highlighted in a printed version of his lecture. These instructions impressed me as *imperatives* and are not simple to accomplish, in fact, both tasks will be difficult to achieve.

It was also of interest to me that Bradbury did not speak in his lecture to us about Death or how thoughts of Death can impact, effect writing, mental health and a writer's enthusiasm. As a consequence, I added more of my poems, following, concerning Death; the last one contains four stanzas.

Peter Kaufman

Hourglass

I cannot *love* you
As a young man
For it is today, and sand
Through my glass
Has flowed
So now I go
At another ardent pace
That only youth can give
Its time to glean.
Nor green, dear, you be
Poised in sexuality
At that edge of genesis
Where all newness grows,
And grows, and grows
Until you know
Our sifted sands
Make still more levels
On which we stand
To *love*
And see the stars.

Daylight Again

It's tidy up time:
Like dead weeds
That grew abundantly
In the seams
Of sidewalks
During the seed Time of life,
And those horns-of-plenty:
Attics, basements, closets,
Garages, with garment bags,
Boxes, barrels, desks,
Dressers stuffed
With memories, stored strife;
All in categories
From a hair lock
To final supplies:
A cup, water pitcher, bedpan
For that day whose shade,
Some say,
Is but the real
Step to light.

The Skiers' Club

Membership bought in grief
Knits tight, tight sphincters
And concentric wreaths
With printed ribbons that speak
The real rules of our way:
'No Trespass',
'No Entrance',
'No Friction'.
And fear, as in a contagion,
Rears its iron walls, its faction
Around us

Fragile elements
Of Time and Health
Grind quietly in the dark
To dust
And still we trust
Do not see: ski dust,
Makes no shared coffee
On the plaza in the sun
With its bright sky and breezes,
Do look up and heed
That still empty seat

Ski, ski, ski
(Don't catch an edge)
As gusts on slopes
Of Buttermilk
Spray powder
More sour than our
Many skis can churn
And there amid the sunlight's
Split, prismatic colors
Kindred, costumed phantoms
Chase, and chase, and
chase the day

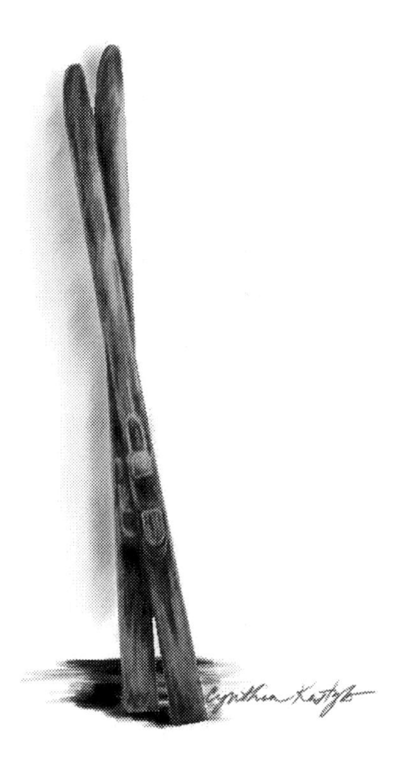

But night climbs closer
Curtails the play
Of rainbow festooned ladies
Who race, and race,
and race away
As if their new sterile motion
Can stop that avalanche
of seconds
And those cucumber sandwiches,
And tea
Eaten
After others
Never after me

Part 8

Addendum

With thoughts of the curriculum in my new class, *The Theatre of Ideas*, I recalled it included an emphasis on what the teacher, Dr. Eileen Bennet, called a Paradigm Shift or Change; when she spoke about it, she read us a definition: *a philosophical and theoretical framework of a scientific school or discipline within which theories, laws and generalizations and experiments performed in support of them are formulated.*

This she followed with some examples that, to me said, 'cultural change;' which I immediately related to parts of Ray Bradbury's Lecture and his use of ideas and images, or events and results, that he percolates in his mind until he gets a direction and starts to write quickly, as usual, about, say, an *entire new world* like in his novel, *The Martian Chronicles,* which according to the definition we had heard, is a Paradigm Change.

Later, I looked again at the essay hand out Dr. Bennet gave us, I reread it; the title is *Thinking About Women, Men and Social Change, in the 1980s*, and found that Dr. Bennet was definitely writing, and included interviews with both women and men, about changes in our society's set of current images of the roles of women and men in our culture; she believes the images are in the process of undergoing modification: a revolution, or a Paradigm Shift, is taking place. I reviewed my class notes and also reread them: Paradigm flexibility is not always available or accessible in our culture because of failure of individual views of reality and often the proposed new Paradigm shift strikes at the vested interest of either a large or minor group of people who have, in their vision, a great deal to *lose* by the adoption of a changed culture; unfortunately, it's often only a minor group which has a lot to *gain* by the change, but with proper backing, can exert extreme pressure while being fully unaware of the scope of all side effects of what they want. For example, in social services for the less fortunate we can see political interest in the perpetuation of the process of helping but not in attainment of the goal.

I'm amazed by the similarities between Bradbury's and Bennet's Paradigm Change efforts, however, each is coming with a different direction and focus while their sense of *urgency*, as expressed in their ideas and images of necessary events and results, is uniform. So,

I'm including two additional poems that appear after Part 8 which are pertinent.

Yesterday's Wind

'Once upon a time,'
The fable begins
Then weaves, spins
A tale of Princes,
Knights, Squires:
Those who dare
And perform such deeds
As we call, 'Untrue.
Simply impossible to do!

So, cautious, hesitancy bound
We mistrust our opportunity
Our cause our goal,
But then gathering spirit
Reflecting anew,
We posit possibilities pondering
Yet again, again, and again
But a ship doesn't sail
With yesterday's wind.'

Time Starts Now

Imprisoned
In that umbra
Of prior pain
And its darkness,
Its numbness
That piles
Shadow upon shadow,
Layer by layer,
To blot out
Your evenness
Your energy?
Evolve Hell,
Erupt!
Time Starts Now.

Autumn Leaves

Prologue

It was Angie who came up with the idea for us to make yet another change/choice for our Travel Agenda by going to the east coast to see the color changes in the leaves and visit a few old friends of mine: Lewis, Bill and Jim in Connecticut, and one of her friends, Ginger, who lives in Vermont. Lewis was the key for me to see as both us went to Yale, graduated in 1950, and worked at North American Aviation, Inc. until he moved back to Connecticut to a good job in Personnel with United Technologies. Both Angie and I agreed it was right to make the trip as time is getting short and many of our friends might not be here next year for us to either see them or the leaves change colors.

So, we made all the phone calls and arrangements, by-and-after talking to Ginger and Lewis, who agrees to our staying with him in Simsbury. He is glad we are coming as he's due for an at home retirement party from United Technologies which he has delayed planning to give himself for more months than he wants to admit. He even told me on the phone he's giving up smoking right now to be in top form to handle what is sure to be an adventure to remember; that's both our visit and all the festivities he is planning. The last time Angie and I saw Lewis was at the Yale reunion, our 60th, which was a few years ago. I'm sensitive to his comment about smoking, too, since I don't smoke and the biggest percentage of the Class of '50 are all WWII vets, Service buddies who smoked like hell since who the Hell knew if you were going to be alive tomorrow and smoking relieved lots of tension by taking your mind off the future. The list already includes: Tom, Norm, 'R.G', Roland, and John; they are gone and, also, were absent from the '60th Reunion.

We were set to take the very early non-stop from LA into Hartford on Thursday. Hartford is quite convenient to Simsbury so Lewis can meet us at 12:30 PM; the airport is only about a ten mile drive from his home. He mentioned on the phone, "I'll need help to pick up ice for the drinks as my old refrigerator's ice machine continues to miss the morning-report as, Present, so I list it as 'absent-unready for duty'. I've plenty of liquor, especially *Southern Comfort*, my favorite, I got at the Retirement Party at work; it's the ice that makes me nervous," he said.

Part 1

When we arrived in Baggage Claim, Lewis was already there to meet us. I spotted our bags and Lewis helped me take them off the rotating turn table. I got a metal cart to move the bags and we followed Lewis to where he had parked his car.

"Melissa is at home getting lunch ready, and she expects us about 1:30 so I can take the scenic route to show you one of the great houses in our neighborhood that has a huge amount of land around it and the leaves have already started to change colors. Tomorrow we are off to Boston for a tour of some of the famous sites downtown which will include Faneuil Hall, Quincy

Market, The Old South Meeting House, Old North Church if we have time because it is several miles north of the other sites I just mentioned, the Boston Common which is the oldest public park in the United States and the Public Gardens. We'll eat lunch at one of the restaurants in Faneuil Hall where there is great shopping. As I said on the phone, Friday will be the day I stock up on ice for the party on Saturday. I might need some more liquor especially vodka for the ladies."

"Sounds like you have planned a full program, Lewis; I guess the property around your house has plenty of trees, too, that are also changing color."

"Right and Angie can go with us to get the ice and vodka and see some of Simsbury as well. Ok, we'll be passing the special house and property I mentioned; I'm not much of an expert on trees but the fir trees which are all still green, of course, will stand out like proverbial sore thumbs."

Angie began calling out as many colors as we could see and to which she gave names---shades of gold, lavender, rust, off-green leaves in some trees where the color change was not complete, fire like orange, gold/yellow and crimson red. Also piles of leaves on the ground some-of-which were already turning a dead-brown.

"Here we are; I'll put all the bags in the house and up-stairs in your bedroom and show you the bath. We'll meet in the dining room when you are ready and after Melissa gives you a call to come downstairs, lunch is served. We're having salad, pizza, ice tea---or coffee if you prefer, and a surprise dessert. So glad you are making this trip and giving us the chance to see both of you again. Here comes Melissa to welcome you. You're right, Gene, we'll keep busy during your visit so we don't waste any time which at our ages is really stupid."

Part 2

After the delicious lunch of the three cheese and pepperoni pizza, a salad of mixed greens, sliced pears, nuts and balsamic dressing, red wine and the surprise dessert of tapioca pudding, Lewis made the suggestion, "The ladies stay in the dining room to visit, have coffee while Gene and I adjourn to the study to talk more about the plans for the Boston trip, buying vodka and ice, seeing the trees in Simsbury and on the trip to Boston and preparing for the delayed retirement party on Saturday."

Once in the study, Lewis seemed extra thoughtful so I asked him, "What his job was that he left North American for?"

"A unique Personnel assignment to recruit potential employees by traveling a great deal, especially to colleges and universities, to interview students when job recruiting sessions for students to sign up for are held. We use these types of opportunities to search for what United Technologies needs. In short, I figure out what kinds of people will qualify for jobs we have open; especially those who match the UT personality profile. And once in a while, try to spot a person who is flexible and promotable and would fit well into our corporate structure after filling a job we have now until promotions are earned for a managerial or senior level position."

"Do you mean, capable of *change* or are some of the people you are talking about *simply are what they are*?"

"Good points. I meet, obviously all sorts personality types, and for those we do hire I compare my conclusions about them to how they turn out in their assignments."

"And ---?"

"I figure the most successful person, say x, no matter how you define success, does not look to others for results because others may make mistakes; so, x looks only inwards for *his* capable outcomes but then there are also always those who are just *doing what they are*."

"Do you recall a significant personality to avoid?"

"Yes, the culturally impacted types who have complex, obsessive characteristics like: power, prestige, and control which have to do with x only doing it my way, for example, and ignoring the mature level of experience of others around him while he still insists on 'doing it my way' and is failing to understand that time, for example, once misspent/wasted is gone forever."

I sat quietly thinking about what Lewis was saying; when suddenly he continued---

"Another matter, in addition to finding the best person for a job, is doing the cautious thing by not putting a really wrong person in a job which can cause a mess."

"Define mess."

"That's when what seems like just a temporary problem becomes a catastrophe."

I sense something is eating at, really bothering Lewis, and it's *a real event* that was unpleasant enough to cause him to change his mind about telling me about it; moreover, I know he also believes in how he does his job but even telling me what it is, he still decides not to mention a particular catastrophe because he cannot say goodbye to what happened and somewhere there are others who have not forgotten the event---and often remind him of it. *I know better than to ask any questions and figure if he wanted to talk more, he would. I do recall a wonderful book I read years ago by Karen Horney: The Neurotic Personality of Our Time, which discuses the importance of cultural factors on psychic disturbances.*

I did say, "The kind of Personnel work you did sounds complex and very responsible, Lewis. Seems like you had the kind of assignment where a little *Southern Comfort* now and then is needed."

"You're right as usual, Gene, glad you and Angie made plans to come; I think both of us could both use your final observation right now." He got up, got glasses and ice from a small cooler, went to the liquor cabinet, poured drinks, came back, gave me my drink, sat down and took a big swallow of *Southern Comfort.*

"You mean---?"

"That I've met enough people in business and at colleges and universities, to realize that for some, their only dream, their agenda is to live by 'doing it my way' and to monopolize Time and just spend, spend it as they feel is needed to achieve their obsession; especially the ones who have no idea how addicted, screwed up they are and that there will never be enough Time for them to just spend it uselessly."

I recognized Lewis had just given me part of a short answer to the catastrophe that he avoided speaking about and that somehow a person he recommended for a critical position created a disaster. Nevertheless, I decided to explore, lightly, how a person could hold the kind of assignment Lewis has and learn how to avoid picking the wrong person for a sensitive assignment. "Lewis, how do you learn enough about interviewees to recommend them especially when you say, *an x type thinks people may make mistakes, so he looks only to himself for the correct decisions, so how do you avoid filing a job with an x type?*

"Very good observation, Gene; I question carefully promising candidates, check with teachers, learn about personal habits and then *trust my feelings* about the person rather more than only what I believe I have learned from questioning. I use *feelings* because they often tell me what cannot be deduced and, once in awhile, of course, you can miss a critical personality trait. One time, I missed the clues that I was interviewing a completely self centered, stubborn, domineering and center of attention applicant. The result was an individual who turned a good team into a disaster when he used people to *get his own way*, moved from one team member to the next and when he became bored and could no longer manipulate or enjoy making fun of one person he moved on."

"What are examples, if you have them, of habits that illustrate how this person operated?"

"From termination interviews I learned about: being a gossip, reading others mail and computer screens, taking credit for work done by others; anxious to know about private lives, especially sex and just plain sticking his nose into everything. At the front end, I do check grades to see if the person has majored in fun rather than building skills for the future as well as getting teacher evaluations when they are willing to give them."

The more I listened I sensed how Lewis danced around saying what had caused the catastrophe for him without actually saying it. So I said, "Lewis, we should have one more *Southern Comfort* and join Melissa and Angie in the dining room."

"Good idea, drink up and let's go."

"Well, Melissa, what did you talk about?"

"We had a good time remembering and talking about the Reunion: all the parties and especially the big party on the Old Campus hosted by the Classes having their usual every fifth year anniversary meeting, the '50 Class Dinner in the dining hall and how Angie made friends with the stranger sitting next to her who enjoyed observing her low cut dinner dress, and, the next day when Gene took us to lunch at Mory's. Finally, the all Class get together picnic on the Yale Golf Course the last day of the Reunion."

"Sounds like you covered everything at the Reunion, anything else?"

"You tell them, Angie."

"Ok. I began to think more about the Autumn Leaves purpose of the trip which is not as important as seeing you all again. It occurred to me, however, that I felt that seeing Autumn Leaves color phases is like what we humans do but over a longer period of time than the trees do of course. They do it every year at the end of the year in what one could call a life cycle---from birth to death, which for the trees, is their pattern for yearly renewal. I thought how we change colors as we age which is a resemblance to what the trees do and we see it progressing from birth green leaves on the tree to death color leaves on the ground."

"Wow, that's brilliant, Angie," both Lewis and I said in unison.

"Why don't we plan on dinner," Lewis said. "We know all the good places and can set up our agenda at dinner for early tomorrow, leaving for Boston and then what is necessary for me to do for the party on Saturday afternoon."

"Good thought, Lewis, you and Melissa will be our guests."

The phone rang in the kitchen. Melissa said, "I'll get it Lewis."

When she came back, Melissa said, "It's a phone call for you, Angie."

Angie gave me her*, what now look* and went into the kitchen; when she returned she said, "Ginger has the flu and told me we should not come on Sunday to see her. What should we do, Gene?"

"Either we get our plane ticket changed, leave a day earlier to go back to California or maybe we go home by way of Buffalo and see Niagara Falls which is about a couple of hundred miles due west of where we are and on the way to California."

"That sounds great, Gene, how do we set it all up?"

"That's simple, Angie, we work out your schedule at dinner and I stop at United Technology on the way home from Boston tomorrow and have my friends in Travel do the whole job. So, let's get ready and go to dinner."

Part 3

Ok gang its 8:30 AM. Please finish eating as we have a good hundred mile trip to Boston to see Autumn Leaves, historical sites, have lunch and return in time to stop at UT and pick up your new tickets to Los Angeles and the reservations for the hotel in Niagara Falls.

"Angie, I called UT already this morning, talked to Marsha, gave her all the data and she will have everything ready when we see her late this afternoon; you will know that everything is ready, get all the documents so we can relax and enjoy dinner and the rest of our time together."

Lewis planned the trip in stages: north east from Simsbury on rural roads to see more Autumn Leaves and cross into Massachusetts and then go east to take the federal highways straight into Boston. Each segment had unique geographical differences and changing colors as we went farther north.

In Boston we drove along Beacon Street, Lewis acted as guide and local historian as we passed the huge Boston Commons which he said is the oldest public park in the United States, the Public Gardens and parked the car near the harbor. We walked back to see the central Boston historic sites: the Old State House, Quincy Market, Faneuil Hall, the Old Corner Book Store and the signs to Paul Revere's House which is the oldest house in Boston and the Old North Church which Lewis said we might not have time to see.

The time flew by, we did not waste a minute as Lewis kept us at a brisk pace; after our sight- seeing---antiques, boutiques for clothes--- Angie bought a Colonial times history book at the Old Corner Book Store and Melissa bought stuff at some of the specialty food stores at Quincy Market; then we got the car, changed lunch, and drove to Copley Square to the famous *Plaza.*

After an enormous lunch, Lewis drove us completely around The Commons where cows used to graze and then around three sides of the Public Gardens and its pond where we saw the famous Swan boats before we began our trip back to Simsbury by way of United Technologies in Hartford to get our new documents for the trip to Niagara Falls and on to Los Angeles, to and from Buffalo, New York. Angie and I were in the backseat for the trip and, as expected, after all walking and the wonderful lunch, we fell soundly asleep. When we stopped at United Technologies, Lewis let us sleep and went in alone. He revived us in Simsbury with Melissa's home brewed coffee and one of the desserts she bought at the Quincy market. Lewis and I switched to *Southern Comfort* in place of dessert.

Reading and discussing the documents during coffee and *Southern Comfort,* we found we were staying at the Sheraton on the falls which has: Casino Niagara, Spa Services, a unique Falls view restaurant and a unique bridge for husbands, over the falls, to use to walk to the Canadian side while the wife is having the massage-facial special at the spa. Also, our plane leaves Buffalo in the morning at 10 AM to arrive at LAX at noon because of the time difference in our favor; we continued the discussion about Saturday, before the Long Delayed Retirement party, how to be ready for it, by starting Lewis's errands about 9 AM when everything is open.

Part 4

After coffee, Lewis and I set out to buy ice, Vodka and Cosmopolitan Mix for the ladies. Between stops, Lewis began to express thoughts about our visit and buying ice and the other stuff, "I don't really need all the ice, no doubt there will be plenty left over, I just wanted to get out of the house and talk some more with you, Gene. Angie dwells more on the end of life with the Autumn

Leaves; I've been thinking a lot about the seasons Spring, Summer and early Fall which is when a song by Crosby, Still and Nash came to me. Nash wrote the music and words to, *Wasted On The Way,* he talks about--- 'Seeing his life before him running around the way it used to be---and there's so much time to make up everywhere you turn, time we have wasted on the way---so much water moving underneath the bridge, let the water come and carry us away---'

I knew the song and also that Nash included '---love wasted on the way---and that he is older now. Lewis continued talking about his thoughts; I think about a poem I read where the poet said, *'Charm did dance 'round us…and we remembering light hearted days, where fun, parties, glorious intimate nights of living, hugging, loving and time, Oh yes, wondrous time we thought would never end!*

I was amazed, said nothing, Lewis was reciting part of a poem I knew; he stopped and said, "Let's get the rest of the ice and go to a Liquor Store for the Vodka and Cosmopolitan Mix for the ladies."

All his concentration on time, wasted time, comments at the airport of keeping busy and the brisk pace he used in Boston told me that Lewis is not well and why he is especially pleased about our visit. It reminded me of my high school reunion in Pennsylvania where my long, long time friend, Reid, was so happy when I came to the 46th reunion, he got to see me and died two days after the reunion was over, and I knew how important it was that I followed Reid's wife's phone call to me begging me to come. Also the waist gunner on the B17G who did go to the Adriatic to see the filming, at my insistence that he go, and relive what he had been part of---the crash landing and survival and the discovery of the nearly perfect wreck of the B17G that was being filmed at the bottom of the Adriatic Sea.

"Ok, let's get the rest of the stuff," Lewis, said, "and head for home."

When we arrived, Lewis told me to go to the dining room for sandwiches, he would join Melissa, Angie and me later after *he* stored everything for the party: ice, Vodka and Cosmopolitan Mix in the kitchen fridge, ice in the family room bar, ice in the small fridge in the den, ice in the sink in the down stairs bath room and the rest of the ice in the kitchen sink and the garage; Lewis came in to enjoy the sandwiches the gals made while we were driving, shopping and conversing.

The guests started arriving about 2:30 PM; the women headed for the kitchen, the men for the bar in the family room. As the drinking began in earnest, the noise level escalated. Everyone brought gifts: Lewis's favorite liquor, a cake and some compact disk music which the one donor claimed contained favorite music (best of Frank Sinatra, Crosby, Stills and Nash and some Big Band favorites---Glenn Miller, Artie Shaw, Tommy/Jimmy Dorsey, and Harry James). Angie came in and joined me in my little niche in the family room where we could meet everyone, see a lot, but not over hear the jokes and UT private topics being discussed while hearing the music on the CDs which helped to make conversation private. At what seemed to be *the* precise moment I heard Frank Sinatra singing, '*My Way*'---by the look I saw from Lewis, it was obvious this particular number was a plant and not appreciated except by a few of the UT guys laughing loudly. After more of the music on the CDs, I began to think part of the party was *turning into, a Roasting of Lewis*; and maybe he was having second thoughts about ever giving the party.

About quarter of four some of the ladies brought in a cake from the kitchen, candles lighted, and Happy Retirement in icing on the top of the cake---everyone sang Happy Retirement to you, to the tune of Happy Birthday to you, followed by: speech, Lewis, speech, Lewis. He turned off the audio on the CD and gave a short, usual---thank you for coming, the gifts, I'll miss you all and thanks for the Retirement wishes; followed by, "My old, dear friend, Gene, who you've just met, came from California to be part of this gathering, he wants to add a few words."

This is new to me, but never at a complete loss-for-words, I began, "Since I've been hearing an emphasis on Time, as many of you are aware, time in every sense is not our friend. For example In Latin, the expression is *Tempus Fugit* which literally means, Times Flies. But we all know that time does much more than just fly it cannot be replaced, it really *disappears* when once it is *spent, particularly spent on what we believed to be important,* time is gone forever. Therefore, I use a very different Latin Motto, *Tempus F-----,* which really says it correctly: Time is screwing us---all of us, and the CD someone brought does say it precisely. It's the CD, *Daylight Again*, by Crosby, Stills and Nash, and there's a song called, *Wasted On The Way.* Here Graham Nash tells us---'Look around us---there's so much time to make up, everywhere you turn, time we have wasted on the way." Nash also includes---'Love we have wasted on the way---water moving under the bridge, let the water come and carry us away.' When the volume is turned on, perhaps you will want to hear the entire song which Graham Nash wrote both the words and music for. Thank you so much for your attention."

It's quiet, not a sound and then someone said, "You Yale men know how to say it," and starts to applaud---then everyone cheers, gets up, begins to leave, the party is over. Lewis shakes my hand, thanks me for filling in when he had not mentioned he would want me to do that; he says, "Be up early, repack, get some coffee, Melissa and I will take you and Angie to the Airport to get your ten o'clock flight to Buffalo. We are going to miss both of you so much, it's been very important that you came. In Buffalo, you both have shuttle seats in the Sheraton transport to the falls and you should be at the hotel in time for lunch.

***

On the way to the airport, Lewis played a Frank Sinatra CD, *Where Are You?* The CD includes *Autumn Leaves which Sinatra sang wonderfully at a tempo that we could clearly hear all the lyrics*. Lewis made no comment after we listened and the CD ended. We arrived at the airport, checked our bags, thanked Melissa and Lewis for the great visit; they left. I understood: *the private conversations with me, the Retirement party, his concentration on trees in Spring Time, getting new Leaves---signs of life not trees with Autumn Leaves and signs of death. Lewis is not well.*

We really enjoyed Niagara Falls, the hotel, our accommodations, the Falls Restaurant and the flight home. We were home two weeks when Melissa called, "Lewis died and the last thing he said was it was so great we got to see Angie and Gene."

Epilogue

The Dance

To question always the why,
The purpose, omens,
Fear, emotions
Of the dance, like each
Bodes disaster, failure
In every motion, movement

So, fashion new rhythms
Of choice, music, color,
Whose ballads of him, her,
Togetherness exist
Not as ill omens of Envy,
Pride, Vanity or Greed

Rather, do include risk, love, lovers,
To stir up newness, erase sameness
And defeat loss, separation to
Inject fun, over and over,
Yet again and again,
To welcome Happenstance.

Juggling a Double Life

Prologue

I call my life unstable as it has contained a parade of events which, when they began, I never believed they could be happening to me. The genesis of the first occasion started in a mess that I still cannot identify the Who, What, When, Where, Why of but everything did occur so the results are always with me and a constant reminder; but how so, Rachel, how so?

Part 1

The Word

There is a word my husband, Houston, used at our fifteenth wedding anniversary dinner at the Petroleum Club which he suggested I look up in a Dictionary; to be accurate and precise, he used the *word* in a complete sentence: 'Rachel, I've become *disaffected* with our life together and am doing my best to accept its conclusions.' That ended our dinner and after wards I did look up the word in the Dictionary; here it is: discontented, resentful, especially against authority.

This led me to the verb to *disaffect*: to alienate the affection or loyalty of, and my husband telling me I am alienating his affection for me and, therefore, his loyalty to me is over. Before attempting to discuss his ultimatum, I resisted the temptation to determine the name of the new woman who is capable of erasing his current state of dissatisfaction with *our* marriage and *me* in particular.

So in the conversation that followed, I had the following points about my personality listed: (a) I am a control freak, (b) an expert in procrastination which is a subtle form of control, (c) a full time mother and non glorious housewife, (d) not socially responsive to parties like when we were dating, (e) need to perk up my clothes to fit the profile of a trophy wife who is both desirable and sexy, (f) I need to complete what I start before taking on a new project, and (g) be more sexual.

I thought about this list: how did it really equate to my being disloyal or lack <u>*commitment*</u> *to Houston and, obviously, make Houston disloyal and lack* <u>*commitment*</u> *to me? So, I looked up my word in the Dictionary; here it is: commitment, a pledge to do something, be obligated or emotionally impelled to do it. That didn't sound completely what I was thinking so I found one of my college books about Love by Erich Fromm, 'To love means to commit to give oneself completely with the hope that our love will produce love in the loved person. Love is an act of faith'---(The Art of Loving, by Erich Fromm, p. 107, Harper & Rowe, 1956).*

I concluded my thoughts realizing that I can only be responsible for myself and that Houston chooses only for himself---he no longer loves me and has <u>*divided*</u> <u>*commitments*</u>*. Back to Fromm, page 108, 'It is an illusion to believe that one can separate life is such a way that one is productive in the sphere of love and unproductive in all other spheres. Productiveness does not permit of such a division of labor.' You can't say there is only* <u>*love*</u> *for* <u>*money*</u> *by Houston, but no* <u>*love*</u> *for* <u>*Rachel*</u>*; thank you, Erich Fromm.*

Part 2

Divorce & Property Settlement

We each got lawyers and the tussle began; it lasted for too many months. It is counter- productive to relive the give/take, take/give that happened. The only contestants that prospered, on the surface, were the two sets of lawyers; the losers were children and the female ex spouse.

The Judge reviews all the documents he demanded: quit claim deeds, Preliminary Title Report which reflects, he comments, 'no debt of record on the property,' then says to Houston, 'there will be no last minute encumbrances,' to which Houston affirms, 'none, absolutely none.' Suddenly, the Judge exercising several unusual prerogatives, awards preliminary decrees of divorce to both of us to be made final when he approves the property settlement. The Judge adds another ruling, 'said home is awarded to Rachel immediately because of the six year old girl and her older brother who, of course, are to live with her'.

I'm stunned, I think, *I can sell the home immediately to have the money for a smaller more practical arrangement such as renting a house in a lower cost area which is really the only option for me and the family, until the other financial arrangement, appropriate to my expenses, is awarded. All of this, of course, depended on Houston's machinations which took place right away when he lied that he was broke, that I needed to find work and no longer could be a-stay-at home mother and housewife which I believed, in fact seemed doable, after I read and signed the settlement that the Judge did approve some six months later.*

However, the settlement is one that is not seen too often; it included the provision that it is a full and final agreement of settlement that neither party can return to court at a later date to change or amend it. I figured this did not seem too bad because of three things: (1) Houston's weakness for his new woman who is 18 years younger than he is, (2) his desire to move on with her and a new life while forgetting me once and for-all and (3) since I had learned Houston owns many Real Property Easements on rural property throughout southern Texas, over or under which pipe lines exist that carry oil from the wells to Refineries. I recognized I would never have a chance of sharing in the fees Houston was collecting---so sign the agreement; and as facts came to light, it was indeed true Houston also prospered in the Divorce in significant monetary ways and why he was behind *a final settlement that could not be changed*.

Part 3

Greed

The pricing system on Houston's the Easements was classic; it was not based on a simple flat fee structure per Easement but on the basis of *the amount of oil passing through the pipe lines* that a sophisticated electronic software program was able to calculate. The money due each month was sent directly to off shore banks and never appeared in any of Houston's local bank accounts. That, in fact, did give the appearance, based on bank documents, of his being of limited means as which his local bank account statements proved! Public records did show the existence of the Easements but *not* the pricing system. So, I did receive what looked like a reasonable support *except* from it I was to pay each month the support for the two children, household costs, everything, and soon, monthly costs would grow as needs increased. Rachel was left with little for personal costs. Unfortunately, I had to agree that Houston had a better legal team than I did. Another unknown fact came to life; Houston had stock in a company that had all kinds of interests in oil, land, Easements and Royalties in West Texas and New Mexico. He was hardly poor.

Part 4

Juggling & Fragments

Rachel knew but thought *what she faced now that the Divorce and Separation Agreements were signed and active, after being approved by the Judge, was more important. She realized it was going to be as if she was juggling bottles, lighted torches, even small balls or whatever professional jugglers did without dropping anything; that is without having a mishap.*

She thought also, *maybe Houston had what he wanted without ever having to juggle anything. But life is rarely without surprises;*

Houston would not be that lucky to be trouble free. However, I am not in any way the kind of woman who would wish Houston a life of juggling stressful problems that might have a negative impact on his relationship with his children which might provide the opportunity for extra aid from Houston directly to the children---especially when a daughter asks for it. Maybe the children asking for money is a hole in Huston's strategy.

As time passed and as stressful as her life became Rachel concluded *life is not about juggling a complex whole, such as your entire life isn't a single, all-at-once thing, but a process of managing a series of fragments, and that she had much to live for like: (1) seeing her family mature and become successful at school and continuing to make good choices, with her input to help them, for their agendas now and in the future; for me: (2) a social life; (3) a romantic-intimate life; (4) a project type business career specializing in contributions to charity fund raising programs, interior design where my knowledge of color, fabrics and space use and layouts would be essential and (5) creating, long term clients who engender referrals in items 2 through 5 of my program so far. Item (6) immediately came up, to get help driving and get a usual massage for my neck and feet, victims of extensive driving.* Rachel concluded, *the key is to manage fragments, fragments that hide the master plan---don't give away the macro objective.*

Also, Rachel mused, *I can't let my career ideas crowd out my love of cooking, music and memories; often it's the memories, triggered by music, that keep us going and stir the imagination to create new artistic product.*

As a full time mother and housewife one of the impacts that came to light at the outset was eating alone when the children were with their father, it was not clear how often the new step mother was with them. However, it was Rachel's loss of Houston when they would both think of the same thing at the same time that was absent now and Rachel could not express to herself how its absence bothered her. It caused stress and more stress was not what she needed.

Part 5

Illusions & Reality

Rachel glances at her watch; she has to hurry to avoid being late. She is both tired and tense now, of course, because of years running everything she is responsible for and Houston being no longer available to drive which is one of the things, driving, she counted on him to do without her expending energy in supervision. So before starting the car, Rachel picks a CD from the collection she keeps in the car to play while making any longer drive to a business appointment. She looks at the cover and cannot believe she selected such an appropriate CD that fits her mood and disposition: it's an album called *Wildflower* (1960) by Joni Mitchell that contains one of Rachel's absolute favorite pieces of music, *Both Sides Now,* which she has not listened to in quite a while.

She talks through the lyrics in the three verses but sings as loud as she can the final lines of each verse: *it's cloud's, love's, life's illusions I recall, I really don't know (all three repeated, one at a time) at all.* After her divorce experience and the settlement, Rachel pulls over to a diner, gets a cup of coffee, and begins to think more of what the lyrics mean to her now. Rachel concludes *that the first verse about clouds tells me that clouds is a statement of reality of how we get carried away and the illusions (realities) clouds represent, (up and down) are really present in love and life also; so the two subsequent verses contain illusions (realities) about win and lose and give and take.* The Lyric in verse one includes that, as Joni wrote it, *clouds got in the way of my way of doing much more*. Rachel thought *the message for me in, Both Sides Now, is I need to persevere but see reality and not illusions.*

Rachel finished thinking, drinking coffee and reached her destination with a new spirit and on time.

Cheated II

Necessity tricked me,
Don't you see?
With its sexual mysteries
That made my choice no choice
Since I pledged, too soon,
Life's afternoon
And became entrapped
In obligation's vise
Where I traded freedom
To flow, to play
In the field
Of the young,
Where time hung
Slowly in the sun;

Did the departure
Dispel your fury?
"Not to compromise,
Not to adjust---
All that money,"
She muttered.
"But, night now ensues
And my anger waxes
At that obligatory vise,
Oh, I was controlled,
Then rejected,
Don't you see?
I'll not be manipulated twice."

Divorce

How brief the instant
Between stress's initial bite
And believed nights
Of simple passion,
Free of apprehension,
Until middle time
With real attention
To separation drawn,
And its monopoly
Of focus;

Desperate, glancing back,
Now understanding too well
How separation's spell
Gripped, and, alas,
The anguish persists
Until, after months of scares,
Pained, who declares
"Who will watch us
Balance what is owed?"
At last, *one* is gone;

And *one* is alone,
The energy account drained,
Aching, aware
The first to die
Suffered departure's greatest
Scares.

Cancun

Prologue: The Garden

Pierre Oiseau a French Intelligence Agent passes through Belize City in the dead of night traveling north on 307, where the traffic is now at a bare minimum, gathering intelligence on the transport of drugs from Columbia, via Mexico, to the US by following a truck of drugs to Cancun. Five hours later he loses sight of the truck North of Tulum at the junction of 307 and a dirt road. He turns onto it, stops at a remote old entertainment structure car lot and parks his Jeep. The building has a band stand and dance floor Pierre can see through a broken window; immediately off to the east is a thick grove of trees all the way to the edge of the beach. There, a lady near the well, using a small grill is cooking and selling early breakfast tacos. Beyond the grill, he notices the beach is filling up with many early sun worshipers some of whom are young women who are either topless or completely naked. The rest of the morning crowd is wondering around the beach, the dirt floor, thatch roof huts that are available to be rented to get out of the sun or for sex-time privacy until the rains begin and the dirt floor huts become uninhabitable and all the people move north to a city, usually Cancun. Later, the beach is completely filled mostly with naked sun worshipers, viewers arriving to watch the nude teenagers who are willing to be viewed every day until rain ends the show.

Part One: The Hook

Pierre notices that the small, dried frond roofed huts, open on all sides, are also spaced intermittently on the beach, and visited by a random assortment of beach devotees seeking to find sun-heat relief or sex-heat enjoyment, as appropriate. The huts are like a version of a Mayan rectangular Palaya curved at the ends through which breezes pass to relieve the intense Yucatan heat. In the near distance, the ocean begins to sparkle in the sun and small waves break inside the long barrier reef that lies along the entire 190 mile coast line of Mexico/Belize; the reef forms both a navigation and surf barrier to reach the shore; most ships or small waves never do.

On the beach a strange assortment of people appears dressed in drab, faded, patched clothing that seems little changed from what teenagers wore in the 60s; they are a sharp contrast to the naked young women everyone enjoys gazing at. A short distance into the heavy tree growth area before the sand starts there are small clearings in which thatch roof huts were built that have chain lock doors and no open curved ends; it is from these structures that the more senior people are walking to the beach. It is summer, rain is over and the Commune is filling up with lay-back vacationers: girl watchers, sun bathers, treasure seekers eager to find whatever the ocean yields, and, of course, to enjoy the local beer and wait---wait until the rains start and it's time to leave the Commune and return from summer fun.

While under umbrellas or just on the beach---depending how long they have been here, some of the naked young women still show their attractive white skin body areas which will soon disappear as the strong Mexican sun completely tans them.

Part Two: The Line

About a kilometer to the South, fishing fleet boat masts can be seen between the palms and mangrove trees. The masts described strange angles because the boats have been pulled up on the sand as fishing for the day is over and the fishermen are busy selling their catch to people from the commune and the nearby area. With heat, humidity and fish, the commune begins to smell; it will get worse as more people join the commune and the heat and humidity increase.

Pierre takes pictures and watches in a rather detached way all that is going on everywhere in the commune. He senses and then confirms a glimpse of a soft purple color moving between the trees. The color comes toward him. Soon, he sees the source; a young woman clad in a type of clothing he has never seen before. It fits her body like a swimming suit but is made from what appears to be soft, supple material. Every curve of her young body is visible and the effect of the material around her breasts is startling---it is like she is wearing a custom, expensive French bra that does what it was supposed to do but without any reshaping, just natural display.

Pierre tries not to stare but there is no way he can avoid looking at this wonderful beauty without staring; however, with his mission in mind he knows it is neither safe nor wise for him to lose attention to his surroundings. For some reason, he addresses the young lady in French, saying, *"bon matin"*---she says, *"also monsieur"*---but in excellent French (*aussi, monsieur).* She smiles, not a self conscious smile but a matter-of-fact, self confident smile and leaves quickly disappearing beyond a small commune store that sells beer and supplies.

Pierre hears the tell tale sound of an automatic pistol arming-slide and rolls instantly off the log where he is sitting---before he can do anything, though he has drawn his PPK Walther, he hears the unmistakable sound of an American Colt firing two rapid shots. Pierre facing his front sees the man who is ready to shoot him is knocked backwards, the shot he does fire goes straight up in the air; another man, half hidden in the trees, is also knocked over but it's a head shot and he drops straight to the ground.

Pierre keeps right on rolling as he hit the sand and rolls on to his feet and runs for the parking lot and his Jeep. He hears the cough of a truck's diesel engine and the clack, clack of tappets. It will be a race for his life. The commune and the fishing village obviously are the collecting/ shipping /terminuses for the drug truck he was following. Every effort would now be made to keep him from sharing that information and the pictures he took. Pierre has no idea how many he faces or who has just saved his life. From the Colt sound, he knows, it's an American and a damn good shot, too, just two shots!

The Jeep engine starts on the first try; at the same instant, Pierre activates the transponder concealed beneath the Jeep's dash---its emergency signal would be transmitted to a British frigate somewhere to the South off the coast of Belize. For Pierre, it is critical just how far away its location is. He figures the drug guys had been so confident of success with their attack on him at the beach that obviously neither the Jeep's engine or its transponder had been disabled. At that moment Pierre hears two more rapid Colt shots followed by yet another two. He thinks *I'll turn South at the 307 hoping the Drug Truck is going North along with the rest of the drug gang guessing that is the direction I'll be taking.*

***

On the bridge of HMS *Ferret*, Commander Trevor Bryan is watching the late morning sun's position. He is startled by a sudden interruption by Ensign Franklin.

"The Frenchman's transponder has just gone active, Sir, on the urgent, emergency channel. We've asked the American Orion aircraft if they can give us its longitude and latitude."

"Very good, Number One, bring everyone to alert status and ask the SAS team leader to report to me. Let me know, as well, the minute we have a fix on the position."

"Roger, Sir."

Commander Bryan disliked these waters: the long reef, lack of depth that rather makes navigation tricky and for all he currently knows, the *Ferret* could be headed in the wrong direction. Hopefully, he thought, *we are moving toward a man who is known for courage but, at this moment, needs our help in a very urgent way.* The Commander bends over the chart they are using now looking for openings in the reef between their location and possible reef openings both to the North and to the South. Their charts, of course, are those made by the Royal Navy when Belize was British Honduras.

"You wished to see me, Commander."

"Yes, Major Gloster. We are receiving signals on the extreme urgency channel from the French Agent who is following the drug shipment north from Guatemala through Belize and on to an unknown destination somewhere in Mexico. I want your Royal Marines ready as you may have to go in and get him: probably using our tenders because of the reef."

"Very good, Commander, we'll be ready."

"Excuse me, Sir, the Americans now have a fix; the Frenchman has just turned south on 307 and the nearest pick up will be our point B."

"Thank you, Number One, what time is sunset today?"

"At 1830 hours, Sir, but it's just after 1200 hours now and by arrival time at Point B we may be too late to help."

***

Pierre turned onto 307 when he saw exactly what he hoped for, a man flagging him to stop who had to be a member of American Special Forces. Pierre stopped.

"You will be safe from here, North or South, Sir, good luck. If you are going North, can you give me a ride to Cancun, my name is Jesse; no questions please."

***

"News, Ensign?"

"Yes, Sir; The Americans report the French Agent is safe and now on his way to Cancun. The truck is in American hands and no former delivery personnel are available for questioning or reassignment."

Part Three: The Sinker

Pierre sat on the beach in front of the Omni Cancun hotel where he met an American family in its lobby looking for someone to teach their infant son not to be afraid of the ocean; my job, holding Douglas above and toes in the small waves, is complete and Douglas is a new friend to whom I'm also teaching French---the first lesson is how to ask a person's name, *Comment vous appellez-vous.*

Suddenly, a voice said, "*Je m'appell, Eloise*."

Pierre jumps up, turns, and there she is in a soft purple color Bikini; Pierre said, "*Bon Jour*" and kisses her.

Eloise changing to English, said, "Good day, and please kiss me again. I never thought I would ever see you again after all the shooting at the Commune. I thought you had been shot because no one could remember you---!"

Pierre stops her talking by kissing her again, and said, "Are you staying at the Omni Cancun and would you like to have lunch?"

***

"Will you want another massage, Eloise?"

"Oh, of course, but in a different position; and as I said at lunch, I love tennis and so does my best friend Sally who is here in Cancun and when her husband is away she always wants a good massage, too. She could join us; next time, pay more attention to my legs above the knees. Does that sound okay to you?"

"Absolutely, so, how do we plan this evening?"

"Would you like to see, again, the wonderful smock I was wearing at the Commune when you first saw me and wondered what was under it besides me?"

"Can't wait---but first we should shower."

Eloise got out of bed, grabbed Pierre's hand so both went to shower. He soaped her all over, everywhere, rinsed her off and she got out of the shower to dry and dress. Eloise, naked, waited for him, got out the smock, as she called it, slipped it over her head without putting on any underwear. Pierre experienced once again his view of her, all the curves, the effect of the soft material around her breasts and how she smiled at him when he said good morning;

then she said, "I knew when I first saw you, you didn't have a chance."

"Neither did you," he said, "but you can't go out this evening, basically naked."

"So, why don't we call room service, order dinner, watch TV and you can help me out of my smock, hug and kiss me, and if all goes well, I can have another massage and Sally can wait until another time to join us---deal?"

"Of course, it sounds like a perfect solution to nakedness at a restaurant."

***

"Come on, dear, we should go down to get coffee, toast and discuss our plans. If you want I can have my massage now or later. But really, we need to share information about our stay in Cancun and what happens next," Eloise said.

Pierre tells the waitress "I'll have Regular Coffee and French toast; how about you, Eloise;"

"Sounds great, I'll have the same."

Part Four: *Demasquee*

While eating, Pierre talks about being in Government Service---his assignment is for the rest of the week in Cancun, six more days, and then he returns to Paris for his next assignment. Eloise said she has the same time, type of schedule, lives near Paris and it would be fun, a real pleasure, to fly to Paris with him.

Taking turns, Eloise states what she wants to do: shopping to get a couple of French summer dresses she saw in a window, regular underwear to match, to keep Pierre under control; take the ferry to Cozumel, the island to the South, to see Mayan ruins and sea floor plants turned to coral; skip Tulum which was on yesterday's schedule; and also skip the Commune, dear, as you don't need to view any more naked, young women to compete with me; leave time to practice Spanish; also to eat every night at romantic restaurants that you pick out; and, of course, plenty of massages and showers."

"Sounds perfect, count me in on the whole program. I will have to make a single stop for information, tickets, money, and a firm flight schedule."

Eloise insists Pierre help pick out the colors of the dresses, underwear he likes when she tries it on the fitting room and especially the French Toulon Dressing Gown she pretends is to wear to watch TV. They have so much fun with all their activities and about claiming they are making memories, right now, based on their experiences.

***

When they get off the plane at de Galle airport in Paris, Eloise's parents are there to meet them and her mother, Cynthia, knows immediately that her daughter has found the *right one*; she hugs Pierre with passion and said, "When?"

Eloise said, "Next week."

Cynthia said, "Did you buy Honeymoon clothes?"

"Of course, I even had Pierre view and approve all the purchases."

Pierre thinks *it's Happenstance, I never had a chance.*

A Cancun Theorem

One, add one, lasting
Two, add hype, fleeting
Absent its ethical norm.

Pervasive reality reveals
Persistent correct form,
Adds loyalty, conformity
For mathematical symmetry.

Inner Conflicts

Prologue

There are executives today who seek only employees who are winners and are determined to eliminate all losers because the total of an entity is the sum of its parts. So in new businesses, key officers review their work force to achieve maximum results by weeding losers from winners: these officers usually disagree on conclusions among themselves but it is always select employees who receive either thumbs up or thumbs down ratings.

This practice depends greatly on bias, prejudice, or just plain like or dislike, but therefore, to analyze the present work, effort, output or achievement of others is one thing, but to develop a new rationale, philosophy or method, and then judge *its* output is indeed quite another task. The world is filled with analyzers who would have us believe that it is only their analysis and rearrangement of the effort of others that has real value.

Of equal interest, however, is the analyzer's belief, sustained by his mission and undetected rationalizations, that it is only *his function which orders and ordains the personal destiny of fellow men and events* so that just he can predict and verify a winner or a non winner---a looser: example, the unexpected failure by a consistent winner, often a person who has achieved, at say, the age of fifty+---like in golf or business.

'A belief in a basic conflict within the human personality is ancient and plays a prominent role in various religions and philosophies.' *OUR INNER CONFLICTS*, Karen Horney, M.D., W.W. Norton & Company, Inc. 1945, p. 37ff.

The Cast

Bud Minutiae, CEO, Nitpicking Limited, LLP
Paul Hartmann, Consulting Psychologist
Innocent Employees, Any Company

Part 1

After several interviews with Bud Minutiae, Paul Hartmann realized he had not been hired to identify winners or losers but to locate employees, at any level of responsibility, that Bud could not dominate or who impacted profitability; but it's individuals that Bud simply dislikes because they are simple threats to any one of his conscious conflicts: attitude, control, values or prejudices.

Paul saw Bud's conflicts as inconsistent behavior, like trying to get rid of valuable people who contribute to corporate success, just because they are at an age he had a profound dislike for (age 50+). Paul thought *Bud's dislike is a hostile reaction and he wants to absent himself from these employees by eliminating them. Of course, his action would appear to increase profitability as would firing any lower level cost personnel.*

The debates Paul had with Bud over certain firings made Paul consider he was not being professional, just wearing a mask because to do otherwise might threaten the job he needed badly by making Bud uneasy and also because now it's Paul not accepting Bud's dominating propensity; and this would also focus on Paul's not accepting Bud's conscious conflict resolution about control. Sure, Paul thought *I'm following most of the goals Bud laid out for me but I don't believe in him as a source of wisdom, and know I don't dare cross an authoritarian Boss like Bud Minutiae.*

Further talks with Bud, however, began to show me how separated he had become from anyone around him, and that included me; I knew if I became a threat to his unconscious habit to be alone, just by himself, my assignment here as a consulting Psychologist was over. Bud was not only rejecting my suggestions, but he was no longer even polite about it. Obviously, my ideas did not coincide with his set of values.

I asked myself *why was I being so stupid---just dumb up, ease by, become a better actor; what was I thinking? The answer was really clear: only be anxious to please, fill out my time and be on my way. I realized what is discouraging, often, about the business environment is the price a typical, or even special employee pays in living through the process some executives go through: it's really a constant demand that any employee must endure being a goat while the executive experiments in learning to manage; put one man in absolute power to run a hundred or more people, and he can wreck unexpected damage without the slightest awareness of what he is doing.*

I considered, *could it be that I looked at things more in an individual sense and less as people are just employees who are only worth so much in exchange, as Bud does, like assets and resources are, to be used in specific functions and if things change you do something about the assets or resources you are using; it wasn't normal for me to see individuals as mere exchangeable entities, to me, people are quite real as individuals not just useful production units that are rotated just because of age.*

I was aware that Bud constantly was withdrawing from people and that some-how I had become a buffer that he tolerated even though he had a crucial need for closeness which it would appear he denied; my phone rang, it was Sarah, Bud's secretary, he wants to see you tomorrow at 2:30 in his office---don't be late he hates to be kept waiting."

Part 2

"Come in, Paul, I'm glad you are available so I can review all you have accomplished; please sit down."

"Thank you, Bud."

"As you are aware, I'm usually in private meetings which isolate me a great deal of the time from day-to-day management activities which gives me the freedom I need to look for opportunities to increase my profitability. First, I want to thank you for all the personnel replacements in Senior Staff that you accomplished, under my direction, of course, and I want you to know you have received full credit for all terminations, the last one to occur is later this afternoon; and all necessary terminations are complete. Change is not my preference so your help was essential and removes the need for future long-term actions to be directed by me."

"Thanks again, Bud."

"Second, it's no secret, I plan to marry, no date set yet, but I'll include you in the list of attendees when plans are firm."

"Congratulations, Bud, your marriage is good news."

"Third, I've been thinking of another assignment I know you will enjoy as you will have more independence doing it once I've set out all the parameters and reviewed in detail my directions for my goals in the project. I'll go over all this when my mind is made up and Sarah has everything typed up for me to review, step by step, as I present it to you later; I'll be in touch. Do you have any questions?"

"Just that I am pleased my efforts, so far, met your approval and you have a project in mind for future profit."

"Good, Paul, let me conclude by adding that I believe you worked well with simplicity in your over-all performance, kept me aggressively in charge and you did not annoy me with any unwanted advice. I'll be in touch when I need to meet with you again as I have to leave now with the last senior level termination scheduled for today, Friday. In the mean time, you should take a well earned week off starting next Monday and enjoy a vacation."

"Thanks again for the compliment and the approval of a one week vacation."

I went back to my office well prepared with *the real news* behind Bud's comments at the meeting: (1) he has no marriage in his immediate plans,(2) he is leaving right now so that it fits the charade that I am responsible for the senior staff terminations,(3) the *start* of my week's vacation is the *end* of my employment here,(4) Sarah will have my final paycheck ready when I return a *week* from Monday,(5) no doubt Bud will have a new *consultant* on board, right here in this small office, come *next Monday,* when: my *vacation starts* and employment end simultaneously,(6) Super Aggressive Bud is still totally in charge and ready to stretch his definitions of Honesty and Fairness to the limit,(7) Bud will continue to reduce labor costs with additional firings to satisfy his greed for a *well-earned salary* increase, and finally,(8) I will complete packing my personal property, private notes and be out of here as soon as Bud's departure is verified; I feel sorry for the half dozen low-paid employees in the small Print Shop who are, obviously, the next target for payroll reduction to be accomplished by the new *consultant.*

I put my two small boxes on the floor in the little closet where I hang my coat and walked over to the Contract Personnel office knowing Bud would soon arrive to see I didn't leave early but would be there for the firing of the final older staff employee to be eliminated; firing was important because that meant retirement pension would be reduced.

As expected Bud arrived, I turned my head away so he was not aware that I had seen him in the small mirror on the wall; he looked everything over and left. After a proper time elapsed, I went back to my desk and found a small note: 'Have a great vacation.'

Glancing at my watch, I saw it was 4:45; I retrieved my boxes and headed for my dinner appointment with Harry, at our favorite place, to exchange information and status. He was inside, seated at our usual two party booth and having a drink; he saw me and waved. I sat down beside him.

"What's really happening, Paul, you look worse for wear?"

"I'm not sure that I can be certain about all of it, Harry, but somewhere between Bud's *conscious and unconscious motivations it struck me that the promise of what Bud could have been is gone.* I no longer feel any promise for him is going to be achieved. As for me, I've become an economic unit: simply, according to Bud, I am responsible for one function, firing employees that Bud picks out for termination, and I became the cover for Bud that makes it appear that I'm responsible for the whole show to reduce labor costs and boost profits in a dying company."

"Dying---?"

"Yes, that's the correct word---envy and greed have taken over."

"Then, you're better off out of there."

"Absolutely, Harry."

"So, what's your next move, Paul?"

"Just what we've talked about the last couple of months, I open my counseling business on Monday taking advantage of the week's vacation that Bud just said I have coming---which I know is not true---I've just been fired and today was my last day."

"You're sure?"

"Yes, his secretary tipped me off and showed me my final paycheck---effective today, Friday, *before my unpaid vacation*."

"Well, good luck, Paul."

"Thanks, Harry, I'm going to be counseling all employees Bud has fired and using the money he will have to pay them since he is liable for using their age as the purpose for termination which is not legal under current laws."

"How do you know all this, Paul?"

"Because I'm the one who had to prepare all Bud's termination papers that he had to sign."

Inner Conflicts

A subtle twist,
An off balancing thrust,
An absence of concern
For the terminated dust
That dirties the shoes
Of a CEO in a hurry.

Take care, soulless specialist
Of your corporate strategy:
You don't breathe, eat,
Sleep, procreate or tame
One unconscious moment
That your conscious ego,

Doesn't know:
That another specialist,
Isn't plotting and lying
For your demise, too.